THE HALLOWEEN PARTY

By Lonzo Anderson

Illustrated by Adrienne Adams

CHARLES SCRIBNER'S SONS, NEW YORK

To Kiki Edwards
with love

Faraday Folsom was on his way to the Halloween party at the artichoke farm. It felt funny being inside a costume.

Suddenly two shadows flew between him and the moon. Two witches!

Faraday Folsom was afraid to leave the road and follow the witches—so he did.

"You're <u>supposed</u> to be scared on Halloween," he told himself.

Deep into the shadowy forest he crept, wondering where the witches landed. His heart went bang-boom-bang. Every sound made him jump.

He was about to turn back when he saw something in a patch of moonlight. A gremlin was picking up firewood and singing to himself.

Faraday Folsom followed him, keeping out of sight.

Finally they came to an open place in the forest. It was just jumping with gremlins.

They seemed to be getting ready for a party. A huge pot was on the fire.

The two witches were there. A gremlin mother asked them, "Where are the rest of you?"

"Hunting bats for the stew," the first witch said.

"Here they come now!" someone shouted.

One of the flying witches carried a cage full of bats. She was very wobbly on her broomstick because of it. Before she could land safely she toppled over.

She screamed and dropped the cage. It burst wide open.

"Oh, stupid me!" the clumsy witch wailed as the bats flew away. "Now there's no delicious flavoring for the stew!"

"Here come the ogres!"

Faraday Folsom's eyes popped. How big the ogres were! The smallest was the child, Otto.

"Ho-ho!" the littlest witch shouted at him. "How you've grown! And how ugly you're getting—almost ugly enough to be human!"

Otto looked self-conscious and pleased.

"Gee, thanks!" he said.

The junior gremlins were playing tag, crack-the-whip, blind-man's buff. They were a little bit afraid of Otto—he was so big and brash. He was fun because he was scary.

Faraday Folsom's nose tickled. He sneezed!

A gremlin mother heard and came looking.

Faraday Folsom felt as if his heart had stopped, but she didn't see him.

The gremlin children were dancing around Otto.

"You're It! You're It! Hide-and-seek!"

Otto put his head against a tree and chanted very fast, "Ten, ten, double-ten, forty-five, fifteen. Here I come, ready or not!"

"NO FAIR!" the gremlin children screamed. "Count by ones or fives—give us time to hide!"

Otto giggled. "O.K. Five, ten, fifteen…"

The little gremlins scurried for cover while he counted.

"…ninety, ninety-five—ONE HUNDRED." Otto boomed, "HERE I COME, READY OR NOT!"

He went searching. He growled and acted scary. He found some little gremlins, but everybody beat him back to base and he was It again.

"Aw," he said, "I never have any of the fun."

"Yes you do, yes you do! Count! Count!"

Once more he hid his face and counted by fives. The little gremlins scattered and hid, tittering and teasing.

"Here I come, ready or not!" Otto shouted—and ran straight to the tree where Faraday Folsom was hiding!

He peered over the fork in the tree.

He looked straight at Faraday Folsom and screamed, "A GHOST!"

He ran away so fast he fell down three times.

Otto's huge father hauled Faraday Folsom out, pulling off his costume.

"It's <u>human</u>!" he roared. "Just what you need for the stew!"

The gremlin mother frowned. "It isn't nice to cook and eat a guest," she said.   Still the ogres held him over the pot.

"I've got a better idea!" Faraday Folsom yelled. Thinking fast, he started to chant:

> "Haggity, paggity, klopsy, klott.
>   Let's have <u>bat</u> <u>stew</u> in this pot,
>   Ab-so-lute-ly marvelous,
>   More than enough for all of us."

The ogres were fascinated and stood Faraday Folsom on his feet. Nothing happened in the pot. Faraday Folsom was terrified. He shouted desperately:

> "Walladerry, walladerry, wow!
>   Let it be bat stew NOW!"

He clapped his hands, <u>whop</u>.
Suddenly the pot was boiling with bat stew.
Otto's father was doubtful. He tasted the stew.
"It's fantastic!" he admitted.
Faraday Folsom breathed deeply. "Whew!"
The ogre said grumpily, "I still think <u>you</u> would taste fantasticker."

The grown-ups gathered around the table. The children had to serve.

Faraday Folsom was busier than anyone else. The ogres were still eyeing him hungrily, and he worked especially hard to fill them up before they filled themselves up on <u>him</u>.

He finally got them so full they fell asleep.

The youngsters and Faraday Folsom then had their turn at the table.

When the little ones went back to play, the mother who had defended Faraday Folsom took him by the hand and showed him her family's cave home.

"It's cozy!" Faraday Folsom said. "I wish I could live in a cave like this."

"Well," the gremlin mother said, "I hope you will come to see us again."

"I'd like to," Faraday Folsom said.

"Good. It's a pleasant surprise to get to know you. I've always heard that humans were fierce and cruel. I want my children to grow up without fear. I'm glad they've met you."

On a table lay an Arab scarab, made of gold. The gremlin mother gave it to Faraday Folsom.

"To remember us by," she said.

"Oh, thank you!" he said. "It's beautiful!"

He put it carefully in his right-hand pants pocket and patted it proudly.

They went back to the party. Faraday Folsom put on his costume again.

"What about our ghost?" a witch was asking. "Suppose his people should come looking for him!"

"Oh, mercy!" the biggest witch said. "We can't have that! I must fly him home, right now!"

"But, but—" Faraday Folsom said, "—to the artichoke farm, if you don't mind. That's where I'm supposed to be."

"Off we go!" she said.

She jumped onto her broomstick, and Faraday Folsom straddled it behind her. He was eager to get away from there before the ogres woke up.

Every one of the gremlin children screamed, "ME, TOO!"

"Oh, no," the biggest witch said. "Only this ghost person—I can't take any more."

The second witch said, "I'll take a few."

Most of the witches were afraid to go anywhere near people.

At last the six tiniest gremlins and Faraday Folsom and the two witches were ready.

Now Otto was awake, and he bellowed, "No fair! If gremlin kids can go, I want to go!"

The littlest witch said, "I don't know—a great big thing like you—but come, let's try."

The grown-up ogres were awake now. Faraday Folsom cried, "Hurry! Hurry!"

Off went the first and second witches, but Otto was very heavy for the littlest witch.

The others circled in a holding pattern, laughing hysterically.

The littlest witch grunted and grunted, trying to make herself lighter.

Finally she managed to get her broom to skim along the tree-tops. Otto's big feet almost caught in the branches. The little gremlins and Faraday Folsom nearly fell off their broomsticks laughing and cheering.

At the artichoke farm only the biggest witch landed, to let Faraday Folsom off—and instantly she was away again, frightened.

"Thanks, everybody!" Faraday Folsom yelled.

"You-oo-oo're we-e-el-l-co-m-me!" It sounded like the wind in the trees. The witches and their passengers were already far away.

Faraday Folsom was feeling very proud.

"Boo!" he said, and he thought everyone jumped a bit—or was it only because he was a ghost?

He had a wonderful time at the party.

On his way to bed that night, Faraday Folsom thought of the Arab scarab. At least he would have <u>that</u> to remember this Halloween by, and to show people.

He reached into his right-hand pants pocket for it.

It wasn't there. It wasn't anywhere.

His heart sank.

Then he said, "Oh, well, it was fun, anyhow."

He scratched his head.

"It <u>did</u> happen," he said positively.